TED LEWIN

The Storytellers

LOTHROP, LEE & SHEPARD BOOKS • MORROW

New York

TO BETSY,
WHO LOVES A GOOD STORY

WITH SPECIAL THANKS TO INEA BUSHNAQ

The story segment used in this book was adapted from "The Foreign Wife," from *Arab Folktales*,
translated and edited by Inea Bushnaq, Pantheon Books, 1986.

Watercolor paints were used for the full-color illustrations.   The text type is 17-point Veljovic Medium.

Published by Lothrop, Lee & Shepard Books, an imprint of Morrow Junior Books
a division of William Morrow and Company, Inc., 1350 Avenue of the Americas, New York, NY 10019, www.williammorrow.com

Printed in the United States of America.   1 2 3 4 5 6 7 8 9 10

Library of Congress Cataloging-in-Publication Data   Lewin, Ted.   The storytellers/Ted Lewin.   p. cm.
Summary: Abdul and Grandfather pass through the streets of Fez, Morocco, and stop at an old gate, where Grandfather performs as
a storyteller.   ISBN 0-688-15178-7 (trade)—ISBN 0-688-15179-5 (library)   [1. Storytelling—Fiction.   2. Grandfathers—Fiction. .
3. Fès (Morocco)—Fiction.   4. Morocco—Fiction.]   I. Title.   PZ7.L58419St 1998 [Fic]—dc21   97-15744 CIP AC

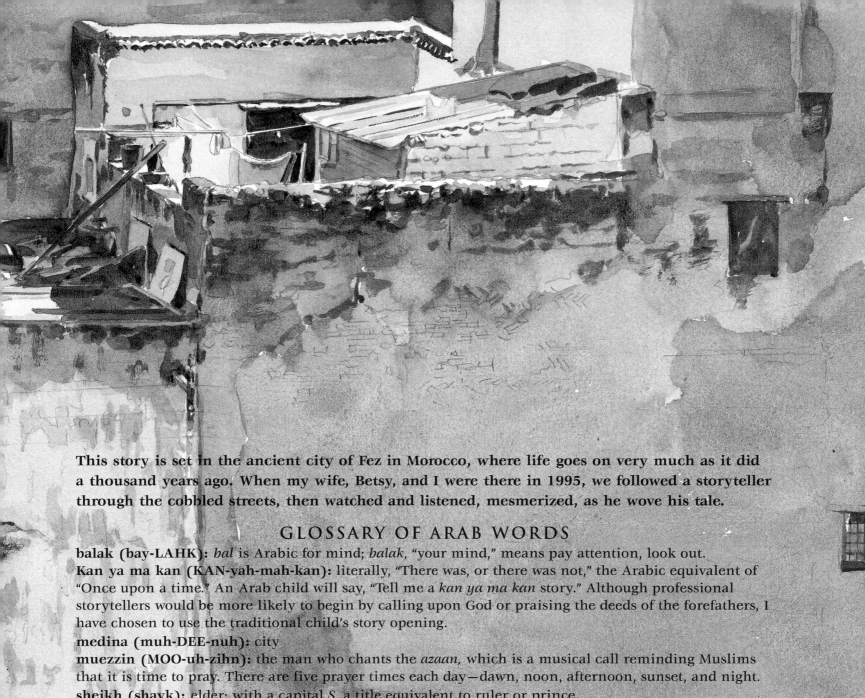

This story is set in the ancient city of Fez in Morocco, where life goes on very much as it did a thousand years ago. When my wife, Betsy, and I were there in 1995, we followed a storyteller through the cobbled streets, then watched and listened, mesmerized, as he wove his tale.

GLOSSARY OF ARAB WORDS

balak (bay-LAHK): *bal* is Arabic for mind; *balak*, "your mind," means pay attention, look out.

Kan ya ma kan (KAN-yah-mah-kan): literally, "There was, or there was not," the Arabic equivalent of "Once upon a time." An Arab child will say, "Tell me a *kan ya ma kan* story." Although professional storytellers would be more likely to begin by calling upon God or praising the deeds of the forefathers, I have chosen to use the traditional child's story opening.

medina (muh-DEE-nuh): city

muezzin (MOO-uh-zihn): the man who chants the *azaan*, which is a musical call reminding Muslims that it is time to pray. There are five prayer times each day—dawn, noon, afternoon, sunset, and night.

sheikh (shayk): elder; with a capital *S*, a title equivalent to ruler or prince.

souk (sook): marketplace. In old Arab cities, souks are covered streets lined with shops and arranged by trade. If you were looking for a ring, for example, you would go to the goldsmiths' souk, where dozens of jewelers' shops are lined up next to one another.

Down the dark streets of the ancient, walled part of their city, Abdul and his grandfather are walking to work. It is early morning, and the haunting cry of the muezzin drifts in the air, calling the faithful to prayer.

Tiny donkeys piled high with brass bowls and huge mules laden with firewood, lambskins, even TV sets, squeeze them against the walls in the narrow lanes.

"*Balak!* Look out!" cries the muleteer.

Wet cobble-
stones, worn
smooth by countless
footsteps, glisten in
the street as Abdul and his
grandfather pass the stalls of
the wool dyers. There men dye the
skeins of wool in vats, then twist and
twist and twist them to wring the water
out. Finally they hang them up to dry, skeins
of brilliant gold and scarlet.

"That's hard work," says Abdul. "Not like ours."

Their old friend Aziz, the falconer, passes them on his way to hunt in the desert. His fierce peregrine falcon grips his gloved hand with terrible talons.

"It's a beautiful sky for my falcon today," he says, "and for your work as well."

The noise at the copper and brass souk is deafening,
as men and boys pound the metals into huge bowls,
trays, and pots, some as large as bathtubs.
"What noisy work," says Abdul. "Not like ours."

As they move on, the noise fades, but now their noses start to burn. Reaching down into a pile of mint leaves left here on the street each day, they squeeze the mint beneath their noses to mask the stink of the leather tannery.

They step through a doorway and onto a rooftop. Below them men stand bare-legged in vats of dye—red, yellow, brown, and blue—dyeing the tanned leather as they have for a thousand years. Then they lay the dyed skins on the flat rooftops to dry in the sun.

"I'm glad we work where the air is fresh," says Abdul.

As they pass through the date souk, a man calls, "Dates of Sahara, how nice they are. May I offer you one?" Shafts of sunlight stab through the reed roofs overhead, piercing the gloom beneath.

"We are lucky to work where we can see the sky," says Abdul.

The souks go on and
on—streets of spice sellers
and chicken vendors and
saddle makers. They pass
carpenters making
elaborate inlaid tables
that will then be painted
to look very old and
weavers clickety-clacking
at their looms, their
children by their sides.

There's a stall full of pots that shine like so
many suns in the ink-dark alley. There are
craftsmen making beautiful curved combs from
horns of sheep. There's the carpet souk, filled with
fine Berber rugs from the High Atlas Mountains.

At last they reach the old gate. They spread their carpet on the ground, and Grandfather dons his special tunic. Then they take off their shoes and sit down cross-legged. Abdul opens the cage he has been carrying. A white pigeon steps out and flies directly to the top of Abdul's head.

Grandfather props an old photo of
himself against a silver teapot. In it he is
as young as Abdul, and a white pigeon
sits on top of *his* head.

He has been doing this for a
very long time. He picks up his
old beaded water pipe, and
they wait.

Slowly people gather, dropping coins onto the carpet. When there are enough, Abdul stands, takes the pigeon in his hands, and tosses it high into the air. Up, up it flies until it is almost out of sight, then swoops back down to Abdul's head, bringing with it a story from the sky.

Grandfather takes a puff from his pipe. The crowd tightens in a circle around him. Those in front squat down.

"*Kan ya ma kan,*" Grandfather begins. "This happened, or maybe it did not. The time is long past, and most is forgot." His voice drops to a whisper, and the crowd leans in.

"A Bedouin prince rich both in camels and in gold had a son he called Faris, for he was strong and well made, like a hero of tales...." The story starts to unfold.

"There had been no keener horseman than Faris since Prince Mohammad was a youth, and a raid was an adventure suited to his taste...." The crowd holds its breath as adventure follows adventure. And then, a surprise. "Faris's brothers planned to kill him in his sleep...." The crowd gasps.

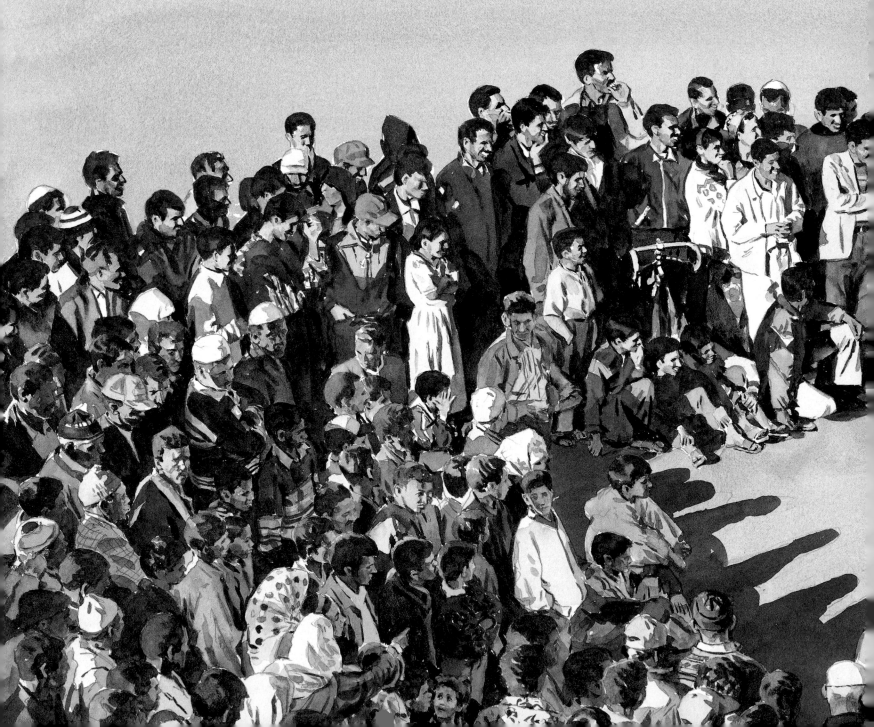

The story weaves on, full of crafty deceits and feats of strength and acts of bravery. Finally, with a grand flourish, his arms raised to the sky, Grandfather finishes his tale. "So Faris became Sheikh, and his fame flew, as if on wings, among all the Arabs of that time.... This story's bird has taken flight; to everyone a peaceful night."

The crowd sighs as one. He has touched their hearts, just as he has done ever since Abdul can remember.

Over and over again, Abdul sends the white bird into the sky to bring back a story. Finally the last crowd drifts away, reluctant to leave the magic. Abdul gently places the pigeon back in its cage while Grandfather gathers the last of the day's coins. Then they roll up the carpet. Tomorrow the bird will bring Grandfather other stories from the sky, but for now it is time to go home.

"We have the best job in the whole *medina*," says
Abdul, and Grandfather nods as the two of them walk
back through the gate into the ancient walled city.